To Debbie and her Gn

Never give up looking you *cmiss!*

♡ Carol 1-08

GEORGIE
THE GIFTED
GIRAFFE

written by Carol C. Jackson
illustrated by George Chavatel

Thank you!

Carol C Jackson

A c k n o w l e d g e m e n t

George and Carol want to thank all the men, women and children
who supported them in this endevour. You know who you are.

To order additional copies of this book, contact:
Xlibris Corporation
1-888-795-4274
www.Xlibris.com
Orders@Xlibris.com

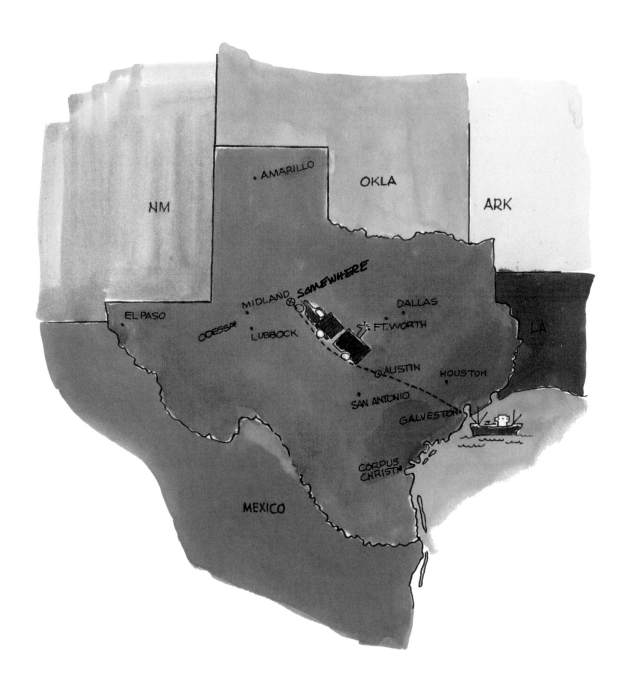

Somewhere, Texas, the animal sanctuary and home of Mr. Johnson and his grandson Bobby Johnson.

Mr. and Mrs. Giraffe and other exotic, African animals came to live on Mr. Johnson's wildlife sanctuary in Texas. They filled their stomachs with the leaves of trees, thick pasture grasses and clean water. They munched strange-tasting foods like apples, sweet potatoes and carrots.

After a few months in Texas, Mr. and Mrs. Giraffe had a son. His skinny legs wobbled and his head swayed to and fro on a long neck. The little giraffe drank milk and nibbled leaves. He played with the baby antelope, zebra and gazelle. The African babies romped with the Texas cattle, goats and sheep in the big, safe pastures of Mr. Johnson's wildlife sanctuary.

Bobby Johnson tugged at his grandpa's sleeve. "Grandpa, where's your petting zoo?"

"There isn't one here," replied Grandpa.

"But Grandpa, we need to have baby animals for me to pet. I can let my friends feed 'em, too."

Mr. Johnson thought about all the new babies. A brilliant idea came to him. "Thank you, Bobby, for being so smart. I think you and I have a new job."

Mr. Johnson and his crew of workers built a small barn and a sturdy fence. Bobby named each baby animal as it trotted into Bobby's Petting Zoo. Children came with their families or on field trips to visit the animals.

The first busy week ended. The workers went home to rest. On Saturday night the sanctuary and zoo were very quiet.

But Georgie Giraffe wasn't sleepy.

He looked over the fence. A bright light shone from the Johnson's farmhouse window. He lifted the latch on the gate for the first time, just as he had seen the people do. His spindly legs shook as he walked toward the strange blinking light.

Georgie peeked in the window. Mr. Johnson sat in a big chair, staring at a lighted box. Georgie stared, too.

In the box people walked and talked. Cars and trucks went everywhere. There were animals Georgie had never seen. Some of them even talked like Mr. and Mrs. Johnson!

He heard wonderful sounds called music. People in the box twirled and twisted to the music. He wanted his hooves to make sounds like the dancers' shoes made on the floor.

Georgie tiptoed back to the zoo and closed the gate. When he settled down to sleep, he dreamed about dancing with metal taps on his hooves. They made a lot of noise. The audience clapped and cheered. A man with a loud voice said, "We have traveled to many countries. The whole world knows Georgie the Dancing Giraffe."

The next morning Georgie ran to his mother and said, "Mama, look at what I can do." Georgie's legs tripped and tapped and kicked.

Mama smiled and licked his face with her long, wet tongue. "That's nice, Sweetie, but you should be happy being a young, handsome giraffe."

But Georgie was not happy.

He went into the barn to be alone. "What's this?" he said, finding an old bandanna under the corner of a feed sack. He put it around his neck. Georgie would be a high-stepping cowboy now. He ran outside and showed his friends his fancy footwork. They looked but kept right on eating.

Georgie put on a show for the children. A few smiled, some cried for their mommies, but Bobby laughed until he was out of breath and fell down.

Georgie's poor legs ached as he limped back to the barn. A big tear rolled down his long nose. He would try dancing when he grew up.

.

Once again he waited until the zoo was quiet and slipped out the gate. In Mr. Johnson's magical TV, Georgie saw a man who stood in front of a large orchestra. He wore a black suit and sang with a strong voice. Georgie wanted to sing like that man. Tomorrow he would try.

That night Georgie dreamed he looked dapper in a black tuxedo. He stood on a stage in a beautiful concert hall. The Boston Symphony played an aria from the opera *La Boheme*. The audience enjoyed his powerful tenor voice. They rose to their feet, shouting, "Bravo, Giorgio! More, more!"

When the sun rose, Georgie ran to his daddy and said, "Dad, look at what I can do."

He straightened his neck, opened his mouth and went, "Awk." Georgie cleared his throat. "Wait, Dad, I'll try again." He took a deep breath and went, "Awk!" Georgie's head drooped to his knees.

Daddy smiled and nibbled Georgie's ear. "That's nice, Son, but you should be happy being a fine, healthy giraffe."

But Georgie was not happy.

He spent the day practicing low notes and high notes. The children ran away from the zoo when he sang. So, Mr. Johnson put him in the barn. By sundown Georgie had laryngitis. Not a squeak came out of his throat.

"Maybe the veterinarian should pay Georgie a visit," Mr. Johnson said to Bobby.

Bobby sat with the sick giraffe. He rubbed Georgie's neck. "Don't worry. You'll be okay. My grandpa will make you better."

A tear ran down Georgie's long nose. Maybe he would try singing when he grew up.

Every Saturday night while his friends slept, Georgie sneaked a peek at Mr. Johnson's television. Weeks went by and he wanted to be many things. Driving a race car looked like an exciting career, but there wasn't a place for his head.

He also liked the rodeo. The broncobusters tamed the wild horses, rode bulls and roped steers.

On PBS-TV he watched the "Gourmet Chef" cook and serve fine meals. The "Green Thumb Gardener" planted flower beds for all seasons, and "Carl the Carpenter" built houses for rich people.

Georgie's family and friends grew tired of telling him to 'just be satisfied being a healthy, handsome giraffe'. But Georgie would never be satisfied until he found his special talent.

By now Georgie learned to make himself comfortable on the farmhouse porch. He let his imagination have fun.

This night Bobby and Grandpa watched the "Animal Kingdoms" show. Bobby whispered into Grandpa's ear, "Do you see Georgie in the TV?"

"Yes, I've seen Georgie's reflection in the TV screen for many weeks. The television might be the cause for his strange behavior, but it does seem to make him happy to watch TV with me."

Georgie's eyelids began to get heavy. He liked this animal program and didn't want to leave.

Bingo! He nearly fell through the window. To his surprise there in the television was an elephant actually holding an artist's paintbrush with the end of her trunk.

The elephant's keeper fastened paper to an easel and spread pretty colors of paint from tubes onto a palette. Rosey Elephant smiled with delight when she swirled the watercolors around and around.

The keeper took money from a jolly-looking man in return for Rosey's artwork. He fastened a new piece of paper to the easel for Rosey to create another picture for a little girl.

This idea made Georgie too excited to stay quiet. He jumped and thumped on the porch, dancing like never before. "Awk! Awk!" he sang.

Mr. Johnson and Bobby ran to the window and watched Georgie awk and hoof-tap on the path to the barn.

In his dreams Georgie painted great masterpieces to sell to rich people waiting in line. When he had filled a feed trough with money, he asked Carl the Carpenter to build a special barn where Bobby hung all the splendid paintings in gold frames.

Bobby sold the artwork downstairs in George's Gallery, while he, George the Famous Artist, happily painted in the sunlit studio upstairs.

Before the breakfast bell rang, Georgie ran to his parents and said, "Look at what I can do." He put a slim stick between his teeth and drew a picture of a giraffe in the dirt. But he didn't stop drawing. He drew Bobby, a barn and trees.

Mr. and Mrs. Giraffe laughed and said, "Just look at what you can do, Georgie! You are a handsome giraffe and a fine artist, too. Never give up your special talent. We are proud of you, Son."

Georgie hurried to the petting zoo to show his friends. This is where Bobby found his favorite pet drawing pictues in the dirt. He ran to tell Grandpa to call a newspaper reporter. Georgie would make them all famous.

*****

If you visit Mr. Johnson's wildlife sanctuary, look for Bobby and Georgie. They are having a lot of fun selling Georgie's pencil sketches and water-color pictures to boys and girls.